Ladies Night

Ladies Night

Anthony McCarten

and

Stephen Sinclair

ALMA BOOKS

ALMA BOOKS LTD
3 Castle Yard
Richmond TW10 6TF
United Kingdom
www.almabooks.com

Ladies Night first published by Alma Books Ltd in 2017
The first UK production of the play was at the Oldham, Coliseum, in 1989

Title lettering by Birgit Himmelstoß Grafik Design

Printed in Great Britain by CPI Group (UK) Ltd, Croydon CR0 4YY

ISBN: 978-0-7145-4384-0

Application for performance (professional or amateur) must be made
prior to rehearsal to:

Casarotto Ramsay & Associates Ltd
7–12 Noel Street
London W1F 8GQ
England

except in the US and Canada, where rights are handled by:

Paradigm
360 Park Avenue South
16th Floor
New York, NY 10010
United States

or in New Zealand and Australia, where rights are handled by:

Playmarket
PO Box 9767
Wellington 6141
New Zealand

No Performance may take place unless a license has been obtained.

Ladies Night

CHARACTERS

GRAHAM   *Fortyish, crass, opinionated, loud*

NORMAN   *Thirties, shy, deeply moral*

RICKY   *Thirties, body builder, ultra-masculine, black, Caribbean ancestry.*

FRANK   *Middle-aged bar owner, ex professional comic*

CRAIG   *Thirties, handsome, cocky, fancies himself as an entrepreneur*

BARRY   *Thirties, married with a son, dreams of being a rock guitarist*

GAVIN   *Thirties, overweight, still lives with his mother*

DAWN   *Thirtyish, ex professional dancer who now teaches for a living. Tough, confident, attractive*

The action takes place in Frank's pub on the outskirts of Liverpool. It was once a successful watering hole, but the recession, smoking ban, etc. have contributed to its now rather run-down appearance.

There is still a "show room", which Frank rents out for functions, hen nights, etc.

ACT ONE

Lights up on the old snug room of the pub, deserted except for FRANK, *the owner, who is on the phone. In the background we hear music and a rowdy crowd in the adjoining "show room".*

FRANK: [*On phone*] Yeah, it's a fair-sized room... Come in for a drink and I'll show you around... Well, the hire charge depends on how... [*The noise off becomes deafening*] Sorry, I'll have to call you back. [*He switches off phone as* GRAHAM, BARRY, NORMAN *and* RICKY *burst into the room*] What the f...

BARRY: Sorry, Frank...

GRAHAM: [*Gesturing back*] Sod off!

NORMAN: F-f-f-Fascists!

FRANK: What the hell's happened? Ricky, what's going on in there? Get back behind that bar.

RICKY: Sorry, boss, but there's a riot out there.

FRANK: [*To others*] Oh, God, you tossers. [*To* RICKY, *pointing at* BARRY] Get him cleaned up. [*As he exits shouts to crowd*] OK, OK let's have some order here!

RICKY: [*To* BARRY] Let's have a look.

BARRY: Ow, shit. Careful!

RICKY: It's only a little cut on your lip. I'll get some ice – just clean it up.

BARRY: Never mind my lip. Look at my guitar. It's wrecked. Six hundred quid's worth!

NORMAN: B-b-bastards!

GRAHAM: Morons! [*To* BARRY] Your singing wasn't that bad.

[GAVIN *enters, eating crisps*]

GAVIN: Oh, here you are. What happened?

GRAHAM: Where the hell were you?

GAVIN: I nipped into the gents before Barry started to sing, and when I came out tables and chairs had been chucked around, bottles smashed and you'd all disappeared. Not your normal "Open Mike" night is it? So you didn't go down too well then?

BARRY: Oh, fuck off!

RICKY: [*Brings him ice*] Here.

NORMAN: He didn't even get s-s-started.

GAVIN: What?

[*More noise from the other room as* CRAIG *enters*]

CRAIG: What a cock-up!

BARRY: Have you got my cash?

CRAIG: You're joking, aren't you?

BARRY: No, where's my cut?

CRAIG: You didn't sing!

BARRY: I didn't get the chance.

CRAIG: You didn't sing. If you didn't sing, how am I supposed to get your cut of the take?

GRAHAM: So how are we going to get reimbursed?

NORMAN: I need my ten quid back. Craig?

CRAIG: Ask Mike Tyson here! [*Points at* BARRY]

BARRY: I was provoked, right?

CRAIG: Oh, come on, you get one little heckle and you twat the guy.

BARRY: Did you hear what he said?

CRAIG: He asked you where you were from.

NORMAN: Not much of a heckle.

BARRY: I told him "Southport".

CRAIG: Then the guy shouts back, "Only whores and football players come from Southport."

BARRY: I told him, "Hey, watch it you, my mother comes from Southport!"

CRAIG: ...To which the guy replies, "Oh yeah, what team's she play for?" Ha! Ha!

GRAHAM: Hang on, Craig. The deal was we come and support Barry, fill a few seats for him and afterwards we get our money back.

BARRY: Craig promised that, not me.

[FRANK *comes in from the other room*]

FRANK: Right, that's it, you lot are barred!

ALL: Oh, come on...

FRANK: I've just had to clear that hall. Do you know how much money I'll lose tonight? If it had got any worse I'd have lost my licence as well. You're a fucking liability, you lot!

RICKY: But you can't bar them, Frank.

FRANK: And where the fuck were you? You're supposed to be using your muscles to control those apes out there. Bloody useless prat you turned out to be! What the hell happened anyway?

GRAHAM: It was quite funny, really.

BARRY: Funny?!

GRAHAM: Barry gets up to sing and he—

CRAIG: I put my credibility on the line here.

BARRY: What credibility?

CRAIG: Record deal in the pipeline. I got a talent scout in here tonight.

BARRY: Where was he?

CRAIG: In the corner, by the dartboard.

RICKY: That was a talent scout? He looked like a dosser. I was going to chuck him out.

BARRY: Talent scout! [*To* CRAIG] You're full of shit!

GRAHAM: Barry was just about to start when—

CRAIG: That's the thanks I get for trying to launch a mate's showbiz career.

RICKY: Actually, Craig, I'm not sure singing a few Bryan Adams songs at the Open Mike night in this dump is the fast track to superstardom.

FRANK: Watch it – this dump pays for your gym fees, Mr Muscles! And you never know what could happen on these nights. We had the X-Factor lot in here last year.

NORMAN: What, Simon C-c-cowell – Cheryl C-c-cole?

FRANK: Well, not Cowell himself…

GAVIN: Oh, so one of his flunkies up from London – and Cheryl Cole's ugly cousin!

CRAIG: Frank's right – you never know.

GRAHAM: So anyway, Barry gets up and says he's written this song about his wife and a heckler shouts out: "I've had her, she's a minger." And that was it – Barry went mental.

CRAIG: Total cock-up. Ricky, get us some beer in, will you?

FRANK: I've told you – you're all barred.

GAVIN: Oh, come on, Frank, look at this place. You can't afford to turn customers away these days. That smoking ban was the final nail in your coffin.

GRAHAM: Yeah, you can't afford to turn down hard cash.

FRANK: What cash? You tossers haven't got a penny between you. Ricky's the only one with a regular job – thanks to me.

GAVIN: Excuse me!

FRANK: Oh yes, I forgot, George Clooney here earns a few bob emptying pisspots at the old people's home. You'll be on the top hundred Merseyside earners' list next year!

RICKY: If you let me serve them, you can take it out of my wages – just this once.

FRANK: Ricky, you're a mug. Oh, go on then – you're right, I need to sell all the ale I can. I wouldn't turn Al Qaeda away at the moment. [*He exits*]

[*As* RICKY *goes behind bar to pull pints, the others settle down.* CRAIG *plays with his mobile phone.* NORMAN *picks up a copy of the* Echo]

GRAHAM: Come on then, Norman. Tell us the latest news.

NORMAN: I'm not reading the news. I'm looking for a job.

BARRY: Good luck. And if you find anything, be sure to pass it on to the rest of us. I'm fed up with signing on, trying to keep a wife and a kid on handouts.

GRAHAM: Well, at least your Denise's got a job.

BARRY: Yeah, and some expensive hobbies, so there's not much coming in from her. And she says if I don't make some money soon she's going to find herself a man who does. And little Liam wants new roller-skates. I told him to go and nick a pair from JD Sports. He laughed – little bugger thought I was joking!

GRAHAM: [*To* NORMAN] Give us that paper, I'll find you a job.

BARRY: Six bloody months since we were laid off...

13

NORMAN: Is that all? It feels like s-s-six years.

BARRY: I tell you, I'm getting desperate. I'd do anything now.

GRAHAM: Talking of doing anything. Look at this:

"Coming to Liverpool later this year direct from London's West End. The Dreamboys. Recognized as the UK's biggest and hottest male strip show, Dreamboys is an exclusive evening for women who appreciate the perfect male physique performed by bronzed, muscular guys who entertain their female audience by acting out their secret fantasies."

Tickets £25 each. There we go, twenty-five quid to see some Dream Boys – Gay Boys more like – getting naked and waving their knackers around.

BARRY: Oh God, yes, Denise went over to Manchester with some girls from work to see them last year. She said the women were like bitches on heat. Mind you, Denise had calmed down by the time she got home, I seem to remember!

CRAIG: Show me that ad. [*Reads*] "For Ladies Only." I doubt it. Look at them. All oiled-up pecs and Calvin-fucking-Klein knickers. Bunch of shirt-lifters!

GRAHAM: Birds who go to see that kind of crap have obviously got problems at home – like not getting it regular.

BARRY: And whose fault is that? These blokes make them expect too much – I mean, look at them. What bloke looks like that in Liverpool?

RICKY: Well, some of us try.

CRAIG: But twenty-five quid each. It's worth thinking about. They must be making a shitload of money.

GRAHAM: Well, if you ask me, they earn it. I couldn't take my kit off – not in front of anyone.

GAVIN: Well, that's a relief!

CRAIG: You know what? We could do this shit.

NORMAN: W-w-what?

GAVIN: He's lost it. The Alan Sugar of Edge Hill has finally lost it.

GRAHAM: No, he's right. Where's your fighting spirit? I'll be your front man – get the tarts warmed up for you. And we'll get a proper name – better than that poofy Dream Boys crap – we'll call ourselves The – the —

GAVIN: The Fat Bastards!

CRAIG: No, seriously, we're already a good team.

GAVIN: Yeah, playing crap football on Sundays opposite a gang of hungover wrecks in even worse physical shape than we are.

CRAIG: And most weeks we win.

GAVIN: I rest my case.

BARRY: We're talking about performing here in Liverpool, are we? Christ, I can just see the look on Denise's face – me showing my tackle to everyone in town!

GRAHAM: I'm sure Denise has already seen the tackle of most of the men on Merseyside.

CRAIG: Shut it, Graham.

NORMAN: I've got to p-p-piss. I can't drink beer.

[*He exits to the Gents*]

CRAIG: Seriously, it's got to be a doddle – shaking your arse for cash. We could do it. Look [*He mimes stripping. They all laugh and jeer*]

GAVIN: Is that what you call exotic dancing? What was it? "Acting out women's secret fantasies." Only if they fantasize about impotent, unemployed slobs!

CRAIG: You can laugh, but this could be our only chance to get out of this shit.

GAVIN: Who's going to pay £25 to see us waving our dicks in the air? They'd have to bring a magnifying glass with them anyway.

RICKY: Speak for yourself!

CRAIG: But surely it's better than the Job Centre. Think about it at least – twenty-five quid a head. Ricky, how many can Frank squeeze into that back room?

RICKY: Frank would never agree to —

CRAIG: How many?

RICKY: Three-fifty – four hundred.

CRAIG: Four hundred at twenty-five quid a head – that's ten grand, roughly two grand each – say two nights a week, that's four grand a week. Just for wiggling your arses. Ask yourself – how can we afford to turn it down?

GAVIN: But what we should be asking ourselves is who'd pay twenty-five quid to see our arses.

GRAHAM: It's not just the arses they'll be looking at. Come on, Ricky, show us what the girls really want to see.

RICKY: OK – you asked for it. [*Shows his muscles*]

GRAHAM: Yeah, fair enough, that as well! Come on. Barry, let's see what you look like naked.

BARRY: Fuck off. Denise is the only person who gets to see inside my lunch box. But, then again, for twenty-five quid a throw... [*He does his version of mime strip*]

GAVIN: Ladies, I give you beefy Barry the Boy Next Door, and for his big finish he'll whip out his... little ukulele!

CRAIG: This is going to work, guys. We'll need a float though.

GRAHAM: Oh, here we go!

CRAIG: No, just for basic expenses – costumes, posters, hire of a rehearsal space.

RICKY: You could talk to Frank – there's plenty of space here these days.

CRAIG: Good thinking.

[*Suddenly everybody falls silent*]

GRAHAM: Just for a second there I thought he was serious.

CRAIG: Or maybe we could find an investor. Or a grant of some sort. Lottery funding? Or maybe I'd better try for an overdraft.

RICKY: I think he is serious.

GRAHAM: Come on, guys, time we all got real.

GAVIN: I've got an auntie in Southport who might put up some money. She's always telling me to get a new job.

CRAIG: Great – we might take you up on that. Come on, what about the rest of you?

GAVIN: And another auntie in St Helen's looks after the wardrobe for the local amateurs. She could get some costumes and stuff for us.

BARRY: Hang on, Craig – I'm not doing it.

GRAHAM: Me neither.

CRAIG: Oh yeah, I forgot, Graham, you make love with the lights off, don't you?

GRAHAM: Who told you that?

CRAIG: The only woman in Liverpool you managed to shag. And if you go along with us you won't have to pay her next time!

BARRY: Well, I'd rather kill myself.

CRAIG: Good idea. Throw yourself off the Pier Head, or better still, do a Bungee Jump – without a rope. That's the answer to all your problems.

BARRY: I couldn't do that.

GAVIN: Why not?

BARRY: I suffer from vertigo!

CRAIG: What have we got to lose, Barry?

BARRY: Self-respect.

CRAIG: Yeah, and six months on the dole has given you plenty of that, hasn't it? Look, you may be right, maybe we're not what women want to see, but if those poofs from London can wring ten grand out of our local birds, then we could make a killing! Real Liverpool lads – real men with real bodies. Just for one night. Yeah, that's it – just one night. How about it? We wiggle our bums, show them a quick flash of cock and we go home with two grand each. Each!

BARRY: Well, I suppose if we toned up a bit…

GAVIN: If we toned up a lot!

GRAHAM: I don't believe what I'm hearing.

[NORMAN *enters from the Gents, zipping up his fly*]

NORMAN: What's going on?

GAVIN: We're going to be male strippers.

NORMAN: Oh. Nice one.

[*Blackout. Music: 'Gonna Make You Sweat (Everybody Dance Now)' Lights up on the bar again.* FRANK *is behind the bar, working on his calculator,* CRAIG *is perched on a bar stool*]

FRANK: Strippers?

CRAIG: What do you think?

FRANK: You're having a laugh, aren't you? Those beer-bellied mates of yours? Who'd pay good money to see those morons bollock-naked? Well, Ricky might get away with it, but with his hang-ups he'd never agree to do it.

CRAIG: I'll sort him out. And, as for the others, that's the whole point. It'll be different. [FRANK *laughs*] No, think about it. Real Scouse lads, not those fairies from down South or those glossy male models – what were they called? You know, the Yanks.

FRANK: The Chippendales. They made a bloody fortune. Still do.

CRAIG: And so would our lot. And you'd have a piece of the action.

FRANK: Oh yeah?

CRAIG: I'd share the profits with you, after I'd taken out my management fee, of course.

FRANK: Of course!

CRAIG: Think of it – not just the shows they'd do, but the hen nights, stripagrams, the lot.

FRANK: And what would it cost me?

CRAIG: Nothing. You'd just contribute your showbiz know-how and, hopefully, you'd let us use this place for rehearsals and the show room for one Saturday each month.

FRANK: Every month?!

CRAIG: OK, just one Saturday to begin with. See how we get on.

FRANK: I need to fill that show room every chance I get. I get some top acts in there.

CRAIG: Since when? Have you ever had Eddie Izzard? Peter Kay? Ricky Gervais? No – oh, sorry, I think I saw Stan Boardman there once.

FRANK: The big comics have moved on to the arenas. That's why I concentrate on music now.

CRAIG: And I've helped you there. I've given you some very strong acts.

FRANK: Oh, really? What, like that Bucks Fizz Tribute Band? That silly little tart couldn't even rip her skirt off.

CRAIG: Only because she remembered at the last minute that she wasn't wearing any knickers.

FRANK: None of the girls you know wear knickers!

CRAIG: Please, Frank. I've got a really good feeling about this one.

FRANK: Craig, son, you're a nice guy but, let's face it, you're a loser. You've been trying to be this entrepreneur whiz-kid for years, and it never works out. And it's much harder now – even for the ones at the top. I had a good career as a comic myself, and then the younger ones came along with their "alternative comedy" – all that effing and blinding and knob jokes. No fucking class at all! So I got out, moved sideways and ran some successful clubs for a while. But look around you, those days are over. I'm hanging in here by the skin of my teeth. I can't afford to back anything but dead certs. And that's not you, lad. Do yourself a favour. Get a job in IT.

CRAIG: OK. Just an audition then. Give me a couple of weeks to whip the lads into shape and we'll do a one-off show just for you in here. And if they're crap, that's the last you'll hear of them, I promise.

FRANK: [*After a pause*] I need my head testing.

CRAIG: Thanks, Frank, you're a star. [*Calls off*] OK, lads, we're in!

FRANK: You had them waiting outside all the time?

CRAIG: They were standing by, just in case. We can't afford to waste any rehearsal time, and besides, I knew you wouldn't let us down.

FRANK: It'll take more than "rehearsal time" to turn that lot into dancers. Bloody hell, a few years ago I would've shown you a few moves myself.

[*He dances around for a few minutes.* CRAIG *is speechless*]

CRAIG: Bloody hell, Frank, who would have known!

FRANK: Yeah, well, I'm a bit rusty now, but it's like riding a bike.

[RICKY *enters*]

RICKY: All right, boss?

FRANK: God, I hope you know what you've let yourself in for.

[BARRY *comes in*]

Oh, relax, you're OK. You can start rehearsing now. Billy Elliott's here. [*He exits*]

BARRY: Bastard!

CRAIG: Leave it, Barry. We need him.

RICKY: Look, Craig, I'm not promising I'm going to do this, OK? And if I did it, nobody must know.

CRAIG: Well, it could be a bit difficult keeping it quiet. I mean, stripping's meant to attract attention.

RICKY: Yeah, but it's not just my mates down the gym and on the football team. But I coach all these little kids in our neighbourhood. I can't risk anything dodgy. So what I thought, if I did it, maybe I could wear a mask.

CRAIG: A mask? Well, we could consider it, I suppose. Are you OK, Barry?

BARRY: Yeah, I think so. Here, I brought this.

[*Hands over a bottle of baby oil*]

CRAIG: What's this?

BARRY: Baby oil. It's what they use.

RICKY: Is it just us then?

CRAIG: Gavin'll be along. And Norman.

BARRY: Norman?

CRAIG: Yeah.

BARRY: Oh, come on! Norman breaks out in a sweat just talking to a bird, let alone taking his clothes off in front of a crowd of them.

CRAIG: If you guys are in, he'll be in. He'll be fine in a group.

[GRAHAM *enters from the bar with a pint of beer*]

GRAHAM: Hiya, lads.

CRAIG: Graham – you've changed your mind?

GRAHAM: Oh yeah, I can't wait to show my tackle to every drunken slag on Merseyside. No, I've just been down to Coventry. Got a job at a factory down there.

RICKY: There's work in Coventry?

CRAIG: So, you'll be moving. That's a shame.

GRAHAM: No, I'm not leaving – I could never leave the 'Pool.

BARRY: What, you're going to commute? To the Midlands?

RICKY: Bloody hell! That must be, what, six hours on the road every day?

GRAHAM: Seven. No problem. And it's work, right? Just called in to see if you lot had come to your senses yet.

[NORMAN *enters dressed in spandex cycling outfit with his bicycle pump stuffed down his shorts*]

NORMAN: How c-c-come nobody else is in c-c-costume?

GRAHAM: Fuck me! Gareth Gates meets The Lord of the Dance!

CRAIG: You look great, Norman. Now, let's get started, shall we? Let's talk about our ideas for your individual turns, and then we'll work out a group number. OK? Who wants to kick it off? Barry?

BARRY: What? Oh, I haven't really thought about it yet.

RICKY: Liar! Tell them what you told me on the way here.

BARRY: Well, all I was saying, like, was it would be interesting to explore the whole area of female sexual fantasy. You know, what gets them hot, like.

GRAHAM: Well, that's easy...

CRAIG: Thank you, Graham!

BARRY: I'm specially interested to explore the whole area of the bass guitar in women's erotic dreams. You see, I know from experience that some women get very excited by guitars.

GRAHAM: I've never heard such crap.

RICKY: No, hang on, I think Barry's on to something. I'm not sure he's right about guitars, but I'm sure they get pretty turned on by the medical profession.

CRAIG: Doctors? Good thought.

NORMAN: Or p-p-priests.

CRAIG: What?

RICKY: Priests?

NORMAN: Yeah, well, women must get pretty frustrated about the whole celibacy thing. There's probably hundreds of them f-f-fancy defrocking a bishop or something.

RICKY: But face it, what really turns all women on is money – money and power.

CRAIG: OK, so what are we saying? The ideal turn-on for women is a bass-guitar-playing priest with a degree in medicine and a Swiss bank account!

[*They laugh as* GAVIN *enters, clutching a briefcase*]

GAVIN: Thank God you're all still laughing. I thought you'd have beaten the shit out of Craig by now.

GRAHAM: The night is young!

GAVIN: Well, anyway, I'm here in the nick of time to stop you from making fools of yourselves. [*He takes magazines from his bag*] I've done some research for you.

CRAIG: [*Takes one of magazines*] *Playgirl*?

GAVIN: Along with *Cosmopolitan* one of the most influential women's lifestyle magazines of the last century. No longer published, of course, but I managed to get hold of some back copies.

GRAHAM: Oh? I wonder how!

GAVIN: A girlfriend of mine was hoarding them.

NORMAN: I didn't know you had a g-g-girlfriend, Gavin.

GRAHAM: Yeah, he shares her with G-g-graham Norton!

[In unison, the guys all open their copies of the magazines to the centrefold page. In unison they all tip the magazine vertically, then in unison open a third flap of page at the bottom, and finally, in unison, open a fourth horizontal flap, a narrow rectangle signifying that the male model's penis requires a separate fold-out section.]

BARRY: [*Looks at magazine*] Oh, for Chrissakes!

CRAIG: Come on lads, if women were really into these, let's see what we're up against.

GRAHAM: Giant, mutant todgers by the look of it. Will you look at this one. "Terry, our friendly pin-up from Monterey." Can you see yourself knocking back a pint with Terry?

RICKY: Not with his dick hanging out like that, no.

BARRY: That's – disgusting.

RICKY: We're going to need a lot more baby oil.

GRAHAM: This one's got an earring.

CRAIG: So?

GRAHAM: It's not in his ear!

NORMAN: They're all c-c-circumcised.

GAVIN: That's because they're Yanks. Most American men are circumcised.

GRAHAM: I'm not even going to ask how you know that!

CRAIG: And they're all shaved – chest, arse, pubes.

NORMAN: [*Reading*] "A big p-p-penis is no guarantee that a woman will have an orgasm. Many women also need manual s-s-stimulation." What's manual stimulation?

BARRY: I think it's two blokes.

RICKY: Hey, listen to this: "Special myth-shattering report. Poll shows size is important after all."

GRAHAM: So you're back in business then, Ricky.

CRAIG: [*Reads*] "Our society is still scared of showing male genitalia in public. This is clearly ridiculous as women obviously regard men as sex objects just as men view women."

BARRY: Can we stop looking at strange men's penises and get back to discussing what we're going to do?

CRAIG: Right, Barry, good man. Gavin, gather those mags up and let's do some work on your routines. Try a few things out.

GRAHAM: Oh, good, we're going to get a floor show at last.

CRAIG: Norman, since you've already thought about a costume, have you got any ideas about an act?

NORMAN: Yeah, I've brought a CD. [*He gives it to* RICKY, *who takes it to the sound unit behind the bar*]

RICKY: Which track?

NORMAN: Track four. 'S-S-Smooth Operator'.

[*The others snigger.* CRAIG *silences them with a look*]

CRAIG: Take it away, Norman.

[*Music starts and* NORMAN *gyrates, then takes out the bicycle pump from his spandex shorts and starts to dance suggestively towards* GRAHAM, *who is supping his beer. When he gets to him,* NORMAN *pops the end of his pump into* GRAHAM*'s ale and begins to pump. Froth spumes everywhere.* NORMAN *finishes by sucking up some of the beer with the pump, then shooting into* GRAHAM*'s face. This "ejaculation" is too much for everyone*]

CRAIG: [*Stepping in*] Stop, stop, stop!

NORMAN: What's wrong?

CRAIG: It's good, Norman...

GRAHAM: Good?!

CRAIG: Yeah, it's a good start but, well, the thing is, Norman, you're dancing like a woman.

GRAHAM: Like a little arse bandit, more like. Has Gavin been giving you lessons? I bet he has. Just a friendly hand on your opening, eh?

GAVIN: You vicious —

CRAIG: Gavin! Graham, enough. Why don't you fuck off out of here?

GRAHAM: Oh, I'm going all right. I just came to wish you luck. But you'll need more than luck, you sad bastards. Who the hell do you think is going to let you do this in public? Nobody, that's who.

CRAIG: You're wrong there, Graham, mate. We've already got ourselves an audition.

ALL: What? An audition? When?

GRAHAM: An audition. Who for? The Birkenhead Townswomen's Guild?

CRAIG: I've done a deal and it's going to happen, don't you worry.

GRAHAM: More bullshit. Come on, Barry, ditch these fairies and come and have a beer.

BARRY: Who's giving us this audition?

CRAIG: Frank's going to give us the once-over, and if he likes what he sees we've got the show room for a big Saturday-night gig.

NORMAN: When's the audition?

CRAIG: I said we'd be ready next week.

GRAHAM: Un-fuckin'-believable. Well, good luck girls. I'm sure you'll go down a treat. Oh sorry, forgot, Gavin, you do that already, don't you? [*He exits laughing*]

CRAIG: Ignore him. He's a waste of skin.

NORMAN: Next week? We'll never be ready in t-t-time.

CRAIG: Look, he's not expecting Riverdance. Just give it some energy and imagination and you'll be fine.

BARRY: I'll have to know exactly when we're rehearsing. Got to organize a babysitter if it clashes with one of Denise's nights out.

GAVIN: That's seven nights a week usually, isn't it?

CRAIG: Gav, leave it.

RICKY: Look, I told you, I've made no promises.

CRAIG: I know, I know. And I'm not asking any of you to commit to anything just yet. But let's try this audition at least. What do you say?

BARRY: Well, I'll do it – if I can get a sitter for Liam.

GAVIN: And I'll do it – if I can sort out my shifts.

NORMAN: Well, I'll do it – if everyone else does.

CRAIG: Great, so come on, Frank's given us this chance – let's not waste it. Let's get on with this rehearsal. Norman, are you ready to try again?

GAVIN: Yeah, and butch it up a bit, will you? These ladies want one hundred per cent prime beef, not mince!

BARRY: Oh yeah, and like you'd know!

GAVIN: You'd be surprised what I know.

CRAIG: I doubt it. Anyway, come on Ricky, get that music on. Come on everybody, let's cheer our Norman on.

[*Music starts and* NORMAN, *cheered on by the others, earnestly starts to go through his routine. Lights fade. Music: 'Smooth Operator' mixes into 'Horny. Lights up on the bar. The guys are clearing a space and setting up a rough stage area.* CRAIG *is on his cellphone as usual.* FRANK *enters*]

FRANK: All right – are the dickheads ready to do their stuff?

CRAIG: Yeah, yeah, just sit yourself there, Frank. They're all warmed up and ready to – [*glances at the nervous-looking guys*] ready to —

GAVIN: Ready to shit themselves!

CRAIG: Ready to blow you away.

FRANK: This had better not be a waste of my time. Or my guest's. [*Calls off*] Dawn! Come on through, will you, love?

[DAWN *enters. She is a stunning-looking woman in her early thirties with a terrific body and a lot of poise and confidence. The guys are instantly terrified, except for* CRAIG, *who goes into overdrive*]

CRAIG: Well, hi – er, Dawn, was it?

FRANK: Yes, this is Dawn. She's my brother's youngest. I've asked her to come and cast a professional eye over this lot. Dawn's a dancer.

DAWN: Was. I mostly teach these days.

CRAIG: Great!

RICKY: Just a minute —

CRAIG: Really great!

FRANK: I thought that if she did think there was any hope for these gobshites she could give them a few tips – draw on her experience as an exotic dancer.

CRAIG: Exotic? Wow!

RICKY: Craig, we can't do this with a bird watching us.

CRAIG: What are you talking about? You're going to have hundreds of birds watching you, hopefully. You might as well get used to it.

GAVIN: It's no good, Craig, I can't do it.

CRAIG: Of course you can, Gav. Look, you've been working very hard and you've got the beginnings of a really good act. So come on, let the young lady see what you've got to offer. She's agreed to come and see you strip – so don't disappoint her.

GAVIN: She'll be disappointed either way!

FRANK: Come on, wankers, let's get started – we haven't got all night.

CRAIG: OK, OK. Lads?

BARRY: Oh shit. This is going to be disaster.

CRAIG: Come on, positive thinking, guys. OK, stand by. Please Dawn, Frank, sit yourselves down here – pretend there's lights and stuff. I promise you, you're going to love this.

FRANK: Just get on with it, for Christ's sake.

CRAIG: All right, all right. [*Moves to the CD player, presses button*] First up we have – Barry!

[BARRY*'s routine. Music: 'Wild Thing'.* BARRY *is dressed in jeans and boots and black T-shirt, wielding his guitar à la rock-band leader. He mimes playing the guitar and advances towards* FRANK *and* DAWN. *He licks the length of the guitar neck. He tries to get a boot off and his routine begins to collapse as he hops about. He has to sit down to get the second one off, hurrying to keep up with the music. He stands and moves towards* DAWN, *but at the last minute loses courage and advances on* FRANK *instead. He throws* *one leg up onto* FRANK*'s chair and thrusts his hips at him. Appalled,* FRANK *buries his head.* CRAIG *jumps in and motions* BARRY *back to centre stage, where* BARRY *tries to pull his T-shirt off over his head without first taking off the guitar. He gets horribly twisted up.* CRAIG *cuts the music*]

CRAIG: Stop, Barry!

BARRY: Fucking strap! I told you I shouldn't wear the fucking strap.

CRAIG: That's OK, Barry, they've got the general idea. [*To* DAWN *and* FRANK] It was much better in rehearsal.

FRANK: We're not Len Goodman and Arlene Phillips – just get on with it!

CRAIG: Right, wait till you see the next one – he'll really get the girls going. It's Frank's own home-boy – Ricky!

[RICKY*'s routine. Music: 'James Bond Theme'.* RICKY *enters in dark glasses, Fedora hat and belted raincoat. He makes some sexy James Bond moves, produces a gun and mimes shooting people. His routine is good, but repetitive,* CRAIG *gestures for him to take some-thing off. Reluctantly he takes off his raincoat and flexes* *his arm muscles. He then goes into a totally irrelevant breakdance.* CRAIG *stops the music*]

CRAIG: Thanks, Ricky, good one. [*To* DAWN *and* FRANK] He's great, isn't he? He's got natural rhythm, real street cred. [*The others are silent*] Yeah, I'm really pleased with the way Ricky is coming along. OK – here's Gavin!

[GAVIN's *routine. Music: 'I Am' (Mary J. Blige).* GAVIN *comes on in a toga, strutting like an Emperor. He has a goblet in one hand, a bunch of grapes in the other. He drinks some wine, plucks a grape with his teeth, spits it in the air and catches it in his mouth. Pleased with himself he grins happily at* DAWN *and* FRANK. *He ceremoniously removes his laurel wreath, then rips off his toga, revealing a smaller toga underneath. He drinks some more wine, pops another grape and then rips off his toga to reveal an even smaller toga underneath. He then lies on the floor, picks up the grapes with his toes and tries to bring them to his mouth. He has to cheat and pulls his foot to within range. He gives up and starts to rub grapes onto his chest – it's too much for* CRAIG, *who cuts the music*]

CRAIG: OK, OK.

GAVIN: I was only half-way through.

CRAIG: We've got a time problem. I want Dawn and Frank to see everybody.

GAVIN: I thought I was going to be given a proper audition. If this is show business, you can stuff it.

CRAIG: [*To* DAWN *and* FRANK] Great, isn't he? There's always got to be one comic act. Gavin's a laugh a minute. [*Sees their stony faces*] Yeah, well, here comes the climax of our show so far. It's Norman!

[NORMAN*'s routine. Music: 'Smooth Operator'.* NORMAN *is in a three-piece business suit with a bowler hat and umbrella. He struts around opening and closing the umbrella at crotch level. He turns round to reveal that there is no seat in his trousers, revealing underpants in Liverpool FC design. Facing the audience he opens his umbrella and grips it between his knees. Behind it he undoes his belt and lowers his trousers. Retaking his umbrella he moves his feet, trying to pull them clear of his trousers. He then strides backwards and side to side, trailing his trousers, which have still not cleared one ankle.* CRAIG *turns the music off*]

CRAIG: Well, that's it so far. What do you think?

FRANK: As there's a lady present, I'll spare you my true opinion. Let's just say that they're all crap.

CRAIG: OK. So what you're saying is that there's some room for improvement?

FRANK: I'm saying – no fucking way.

CRAIG: Right. Is that a no for now or is it —

FRANK: It's a no for ever – the end!

CRAIG: Or is it just that you're fully booked?

FRANK: Craig! What bit of "No" don't you understand?

CRAIG: It's just that we know there's work to be done but —

FRANK: Craig, lads – I'm doing you a favour. I'm saving you a lot of disappointment and heartbreak. I've booked a lot of male strippers here over the years – those guys, they look great: great bodies, thousands of hours in the gym, and they're all great dancers. If I released you lard-arses on my regular Saturday-night, crowd they'd tear you to pieces and then they'd turn on me. [*Starts to leave*] Sorry, guys.

DAWN: Well, I've seen worse.

FRANK: What?

DAWN: I've even worked with worse.

FRANK: You're not – you're not telling me that you enjoyed watching that fiasco?

DAWN: They had something.

CRAIG: You see, Frank! Dawn's a pro – she can see the potential. She'll work with us. [*To* DAWN] Right?

FRANK: [*To* DAWN] Are you seriously telling me that, as a woman, you found that – exciting?

DAWN: They're different. They have a "local lad" quality. And with some coaching and some decent choreography they could have a unique appeal. That's my honest opinion – as a woman. And don't forget, most of your audience are married to guys like these. They must have seen something in them once, right?

[FRANK *looks at the guys, who grin proudly. He shrugs and turns back to* DAWN]

FRANK: I'm still listening.

DAWN: It would take a lot of work but – yeah, I'm willing to give it a go. Depending of course on how hard they're willing to try. I mean, they'll have to go into serious training.

GAVIN: Training?!

RICKY: Sounds OK to me.

BARRY: What kind of training?

CRAIG: Don't worry – they're up for it.

FRANK: All right, see what you can do.

DAWN: Is that a yes, Uncle Frank?

41

FRANK: It's a very nervous "maybe". I've got a Saturday night free here in eight weeks' time. If you honestly think they're up to it, give me a ring in the next couple of weeks and I'll think about it. [*He exits*]

CRAIG: Bloody brilliant! [*To* DAWN] You've just earned yourself a slap-up dinner.

DAWN: Craig —

CRAIG: Any restaurant of your choice.

DAWN: Craig! I was just being kind.

CRAIG: What?

GAVIN: Well, what did you really think we were like?

DAWN: The truth?

CRAIG: The truth.

DAWN: You were shite.

RICKY: Then why —

DAWN: I've never seen such an inept attempt at dancing and stripping in my life.

BARRY: So why did you —

DAWN: I need the work. How much are you willing to pay me? [*They look at each other uncomfortably*] Well, I'm not going to be doing it for the good of my health, am I?

CRAIG: I'll get a personal loan. Or something. Whatever it takes. We need you, Dawn. We'll pay whatever you ask.

DAWN: All right, I'll be in touch. Oh, by the way, what are you calling yourselves?

CRAIG: What?

DAWN: What's the name of your act?

GAVIN: Norman had a good idea.

CRAIG: First I've heard of it.

GAVIN: Go on, Norman, tell 'em.

NORMAN: Well, I thought The S-s-scouse S-s-stallions.

DAWN: The Scouse Stallions? [*She explodes with laughter and leaves still convulsed. They all turn and look at* CRAIG]

CRAIG: The Scouse Stallions. I like it!

[*Blackout. Music: 'I Got You (I Feel Good)' Lights up on the bar.* DAWN *is alone, going through CDs by the player on the bar. She selects one and puts it on. Music plays ('Halo') and she starts to mark out a routine for the boys, but soon she gets carried away by the music and dances as she once did, reliving her younger days.* BARRY *comes in, unseen by* DAWN, *he draws back into the shadows and watches her dance. He is mesmerized. On one of her spinning turns she sees* BARRY *and*

43

immediately stops dancing and rushes over to turn off the machine]

BARRY: Sorry, I didn't mean to – I mean, carry on doing whatever —

DAWN: No, no, it's OK, I was just working out some moves for you, for later.

BARRY: What? I hope you're not expecting any of us to dance like that. It'd kill us. Forget the dole. We'll all be drawing the "disability".

DAWN: You know what they say. You never know what you can do until you try. And that last session was – well, quite encouraging. [*Gathering up her papers*] I'm just going to see if Uncle Frank's photocopier's been fixed. I've got to run some stuff off. You should do some warming up until the others get here.

BARRY: Yeah, I was just going to.

[DAWN *exits and* BARRY *starts doing press-ups on the floor. He really gets into it, pumping up and down rapidly. He doesn't see* GAVIN *enter the room.* GAVIN *creeps up behind him*]

GAVIN: I don't want to worry you, mate, but I think the bird's pissed off!

BARRY: [*Collapsing*] Gavin, very funny, you knob!

GAVIN: Are you all right?

BARRY: I'm fine.

GAVIN: So, what's Denise going to think when your chest starts bursting out of your pyjamas?

BARRY: You're the only bloke I know who wears pyjamas.

GAVIN: Don't knock it till you've tried it. A bit of winceyette could do wonders for your sex life.

BARRY: It's going to take more than that to fix things between me and Denise.

GAVIN: Oh?

BARRY: I don't want to talk about it.

GAVIN: OK.

BARRY: [*Does a few more exercises, then*] She's not "fulfilled", she says. What the hell does that mean, Gav?

GAVIN: I'm not sure exactly, but it probably means she's not fulfilled.

[NORMAN *enters jauntily, whistling*]

NORMAN: Hiya, lads. [*Drops his kitbag, turns up the volume on his iPod and starts working out furiously*]

GAVIN: Well, I'm glad someone's happy.

[CRAIG *enters, carrying a parcel*]

CRAIG: Hey guys, here they are – your basic costumes, direct from Soho. The Real McCoy. The professional strippers essentials. [*Produces sequined and leather G-strings and passes them round*]

BARRY: You're joking. There's no way I'm wearing that.

GAVIN: I'll try – but where exactly does it go? [*Tries it on his head*]

BARRY: It'd be useful in a riot. [*Uses it as a catapult*]

GAVIN: Are they all the same size?

CRAIG: I think so.

GAVIN: Bloody hell. You'd better give Ricky two!

CRAIG: [*Taking* NORMAN*'s earpiece out and handing him a G-string*] Norman!

NORMAN: Oh, hi, Craig. Yeah, brilliant. No problems.

CRAIG: Are you all right?

NORMAN: Yeah, great, it's just that – [*He takes him aside*] – I've met someone. Someone s-s-special.

CRAIG: Wow! Someone special, eh? You see, you start working, you get your confidence back and there you go.

NORMAN: Yeah!

CRAIG: So?

NORMAN: So what?

CRAIG: [*Taking out his camera*] How far have you got? Get your top off.

NORMAN: [*Removing his track-suit top*] Well, we've only just met.

CRAIG: [*Starts to photograph him*] What's that got to do with whether you've slept with her or not? Give us a smoulder. [*Snaps him*]

NORMAN: [*Posing for camera*] Plenty of time for that.

CRAIG: Listen, in my experience the sooner you hit home base the better. Because the longer she holds out on you the more control she has over you.

NORMAN: But she's not like that.

CRAIG: Pose! Believe me, they're *all* like that!

NORMAN: Shit! [*Poses*]

CRAIG: More attitude. That's it. [*Snaps*] Ta. Yeah, the sooner you score, the better.

NORMAN: B-b-but —

CRAIG: Just promise me, OK? I want you to promise me here and now that next time... [*He makes a gesture*] No messing, OK?

NORMAN: OK.

CRAIG: Good lad.

[RICKY *furtively pops his head round the door*]

GAVIN: It's all right, Ricky. There's only us here. We got rid of the Paparazzi.

RICKY: You can laugh. I've got my reputation to protect. [*Takes off his sunglasses and jacket and* CRAIG *moves in on him with his camera*] You don't know what my kind of crowd is like. [*Sees* CRAIG *taking photos of him*] What the fuck is that? What are you doing, you arsehole?

CRAIG: It's just a few publicity shots – for the poster and that.

RICKY: I've told you. I don't want no publicity! I'll do it, but I'm doing it incognito, right? As far as you know I'm The Lone Ranger, The Masked Man. No photos, no name, nothing. I'm doing it for the money, that's all – not the publicity.

CRAIG: Fine. OK, I won't use you on the poster.

RICKY: I'm not kidding.

CRAIG: Fine, fine.

[DAWN *enters with a sheaf of papers*]

DAWN: OK, gentlemen, gather round. [*Hands out papers*] Craig, Barry, Ricky, Gavin, Norman. Here you are —

BARRY: What's this?

DAWN: Your training schedule for the next four weeks.

CRAIG: [*Handing his back*] Excellent.

DAWN: Keep a copy. If it looks rigorous, that's because you've all got a long way to go. This is just the stuff I want you to do on your own time. As I told you last week, right now I need to do some work with you on your individual routines.

BARRY: I've been working on mine and, well, no offence Dawn, but I've got a really clear idea of what I'm trying to achieve, and I think that any outside influence might —

CRAIG: Barry, you – all – need as much "outside influence" as you can get.

BARRY: But —

CRAIG: Right, Dawn?

DAWN: Right. You all need some help. You too, Craig.

CRAIG: Ah, no, I'm the Manager. I don't actually perform.

DAWN: Well you do now.

NORMAN: Yeah!

RICKY: Nice one.

GAVIN: Get 'em off, Craig!

CRAIG: No, hang on —

DAWN: I really think you should try.

CRAIG: But I never intended —

DAWN: And it'll look better when you do the group number – five fellers stripping together will be more spectacular. And for the women there'll be more goods to choose from.

GAVIN: I think she's right.

RICKY: Me too.

CRAIG: No fucking way.

NORMAN: It makes sense.

CRAIG: Forget it. I'm not taking my clothes off.

RICKY: But you're expecting us – your mates – to do it?

DAWN: He's right, Craig.

CRAIG: OK. OK. I'll do it. [*To* DAWN] For you.

DAWN: No. You're doing it for the group. Now, come on, let's get started. [*They start to get their kits together.* CRAIG *sidles up to* DAWN] Are you OK?

CRAIG: I'll get used to it. No problem. [*Cockily*] I was going to suggest it myself actually.

DAWN: Good. So I saved you the trouble!

CRAIG: I can't tell you how much I appreciate this, Dawn. And I wondered if, by way of saying thank you, I could, perhaps, take you out to dinner and then [*suddenly losing confidence*] we could, per- haps – er – discuss my vision for the group and where I see us going in the future and where you might fit in, like.

DAWN: Whoaa! Dinner, the future? Craig —

CRAIG: Just a thought.

DAWN: I don't know, Craig. Maybe after we get the show on – if we get the show on – we can then talk about future "business".

CRAIG: Great idea. Get the show up and running first. Frank's given me a possible date – 17th October. So I'll book us a table somewhere nice for later that night.

DAWN: Craig —

CRAIG: Dinner on the 17th, OK?

DAWN: OK, OK. Now let's get started. Everybody get into a straight line. Let's rehearse your group entrance again. Ricky, you there, Craig next to him, then Norman, Barry, Gavin on the end.

[*They shuffle into place*]

OK. After four you move. One, two, three.

[GAVIN *moves back*]

Stop. Gavin, you move forward, right. One, two, three, four.

[CRAIG *moves forward on his own*]

Are you all deaf? How much simpler can I make it? All you do is line up, then on the count of four you all move forward, throw your arms in the air and shout, "Woh!"

[*They try this a few times, as* DAWN*'s frustration mounts. Eventually* NORMAN *speaks up*]

NORMAN: Oh, I g-g-get it. It's the same as the Reds when they move to put a forward offside!

DAWN: What language are we talking now?

CRAIG: He means The Reds – Liverpool FC?

NORMAN: Yeah, it's like that trick Stephen Darby does.

DAWN: Stephen Darby?

BARRY: No, no, it's Jamie Carragher.

CRAIG: Glen Johnson too and Fabio Aurelio.

DAWN: Who are these people?!

NORMAN: It d-d-doesn't matter, but when a bloke from the opposition is about to shoot we all move forward in a line.

BARRY: And we all put our arms in the air as if to say "offside".

DAWN: All right, show me. One, two, three, four —

[*They execute the move perfectly*]

ALL: Woh!!!

DAWN: Perfect! That's what I wanted.

RICKY: Well, why didn't you say so, girl!

DAWN: OK, I'll start watching football from now on. Pick up some tips. But for now let's look at your individual routines. Norman, come on, let's start with you. Everybody else pay attention.

[RICKY *turns the CD-player on as* CRAIG *opens his phone and dials*]

DAWN: Craig?

CRAIG: Just booking the restaurant.

DAWN: For God's sake —

[*The music starts ('The Lion Sleeps Tonight').* NORMAN *enters shyly. He is dressed in a leopard skin and tentatively paws the air*]

DAWN: Stop! [*Music stops*] OK, Norman, er – I'm sorry, but what are you supposed to be?

NORMAN: A t-t-tiger.

DAWN: A tiger? Great. King of the jungle.

GAVIN: No, no, the lion's the king of the jungle.

BARRY: Yeah, that's right. It's definitely the lion.

DAWN: Whatever! OK, I want you to start again, Norman, and this time I want you to really take the stage. You're nervous – that's OK, but you have to use your nervous energy – harness it, do something with it. Start again.

[RICKY *restarts the music.* NORMAN *leaps about frenetically, gnashing, clawing and lunging. The others laugh hysterically.* DAWN *holds up her hand. The music stops*]

DAWN: OK. What's the joke?

CRAIG: I'm sorry, Dawn.

DAWN: You could all learn a lot from Norman. Unlike the rest of you, he's willing to take risks, he's willing to make himself vulnerable to his audience. And that makes him very attractive.

BARRY: You've got to be joking!

DAWN: I've never been more serious. Norman, well done. You need to do some work on the actual dance technique, but you're moving in the right direction. We'll work on you some more later. First I'd like to see your number, Barry. Or are you worried that I might interfere with your "artistic conception"?

BARRY: No, that's fine.

DAWN: Good. Ricky.

[RICKY *turns on music: 'Wild Thing'.* BARRY *is dressed in his leathers, wearing the strapped guitar again. This*

*time he slides the guitar round his back and immedi-
ately starts to pull out his belt with one tug*]

DAWN: OK, let me take the guitar, come on, let me have
it. OK. Now, loose, let's go. Follow me. [BARRY
starts to copy DAWN*'s pelvic gyrations, then stops*]

BARRY: For Chrissakes!

DAWN: Keep going! [*He starts again*] You're very sexy,
keep going! Nice, nice, keep going, open up a bit
more. You wanna get them hot. Think about your
Denise. [BARRY *lunges for his fly and is about to
rip down his jeans*] Take your time, take your time,
play them along… make them wait. Now then, the
jacket is removed in three movements. One: the zip.
Two: reveal the shoulders. Three: right off and then
swing it around. That's it. [BARRY *starts to take
off his shirt*] No, no, hold it back. Take your time.
One button at a time. OK, now you can go to the
jeans… up and down… [BARRY *goes up and down
with the zip on his jeans as if he is strumming
a guitar, enjoying himself now*] OK, you're not
playing the guitar. Jeans right down now… slowly
does it. Keep her waiting. [*He takes his jeans off
but gets them caught on his foot and hops about
a bit*] That's OK. Now the underpants. Bending
over, remember.

[*With his back to us* BARRY *bends forward and starts to take his underpants off*]

DAWN: OK, stop the music! Stop, stop… everybody. When you're bending over you've got to – [*slaps his bum*] – keep your cheeks clenched. All together now.

ALL: [*Turn, slap their own bums and say*] Cheeks clenched!

DAWN: Otherwise, what do we see?

ALL: [*Turn, slap their own bums and say*] Arseholes!

DAWN: That's right. [BARRY *is still bending over, pants round his ankles and cheeks still clenched*] And this stuff? [*Pinches his bum*] Shave it! Every day – pluck it, wax it, oil it – get it smooth. [*Slaps his bum again*]

BARRY: [*Pulling his pants up*] Hey! I'm not shaving my arse for anybody. No way. Craig? Come on.

RICKY: No way.

NORMAN: F-f-forget it!

CRAIG: Yeah, come on Dawn. Is that really necessary?

DAWN: We'll discuss it later. Barry, get back to your routine. Ricky, music!

[BARRY *picks up his belt and starts to swing it round and beat it violently on the ground in time to the hard-rock music*]

For God's sake, Barry, there's four hundred women out there – they don't want you to beat them up. Smile. [*He smiles viciously and continues to thrash around*] OK, stop, stop!

BARRY: What's your problem now?

DAWN: My problem, Barry, is your attitude.

BARRY: What do you mean "my attitude"?

DAWN: What's with all this aggro?

BARRY: What the fuck are you talking about? What aggro?!

[*Everyone sniggers.* BARRY *is suddenly self-conscious and embarrassed*]

DAWN: I'll say it again. Stripping is part of the art of seduction. Look, you're married, right?

BARRY: You know I am.

DAWN: So, how do you seduce your wife? You create a romantic atmosphere, right? You look her in the eyes, right? You tell her how much you love her, right? You let your heart do the talking, right? Well, it's no different on stage in front of hundreds of women. Basically we all want the same thing.

Think of those women as just one individual – your Denise. Just think what she wants. Right?

BARRY: [*Mutters*] Yeah.

DAWN: OK, Ricky, music.

[BARRY *starts to dance more romantically, but soon he becomes violent again*]

DAWN: Stop! [*Music stops*] Is that how you dance with your wife?

BARRY: What do you mean?

DAWN: I mean it's still aggressive. It's deeply unsexy and, well, frankly a bit unsettling.

BARRY: What do you know about me and my wife?

DAWN: Nothing, I'm merely saying —

BARRY: Well, keep your opinions to yourself!

CRAIG: Barry, Dawn was just trying to —

BARRY: She's left me, all right? She's walked out, dumped me, kicked me in the bollocks and she's not coming back. There. Now are you satisfied?

[*Shocked silence. Everyone gathers around* BARRY. *He brushes them off and starts to get dressed. The others gather up his stuff and help him*]

CRAIG: Dawn?...

DAWN: OK. Everybody, gather round, come on. We need to talk. Just – just get in a line. Everybody. Barry?

[BARRY *steps forward first and then they all shuffle into a parade line.* DAWN *strides up and down like a sergeant major*]

DAWN: OK, we need to sort some things out before we go any further. And this is not meant to be in any way a comment or a criticism of any one person in particular, but – if we are going to go on with this – you have to ask yourself what it is that your audience wants from you. Your audience of women! You want them to want you, right? You want them to get excited. Which is exactly what I'm trying to help you with. And for them to get excited, they've got to see more of you.

CRAIG: Absolutely! And we've all agreed. We're prepared to – you know – go the whole way.

GAVIN: Are we?

NORMAN: Oh Sh-sh-shit!

DAWN: I'm not just talking about the full frontal nudity. I'm talking about showing more.

RICKY: More?!

DAWN: I'm talking about showing them yourselves. You've got to be prepared to expose your real selves. You've got to show that you're willing to give them what they want. It's all about their fantasies, not yours. You've got to drop the barriers and make a real connection with your audience. You've got to make them love you – so come on, let's get on with it.

NORMAN: I'm sorry, b-b-but I'm not going all the way.

RICKY: Me neither.

DAWN: Oh, God! OK, so you're totally inhibited, let's start with that. If taking your own clothes off is such a big deal, then let's do something completely different. I want you all to pair up and take each other's clothes off.

ALL: What? No way.

GAVIN: Lads. Dawn's trying to help us, OK?

DAWN: Thank you, Gavin, I'll work with you.

GAVIN: What?

DAWN: Everyone else, partner up.

CRAIG: OK, you heard her. Partner up.

[DAWN *goes and puts the music on: 'I Gotta Feeling'*]

BARRY: I can tell you now, this isn't going to help one bit.

RICKY: And I'm telling you – if anybody ever talks about this outside this room, they're dead!

[BARRY *is with* CRAIG, NORMAN *is with* RICKY, GAVIN *is with* DAWN]

DAWN: Now, everybody, just follow me. Easy. [*She stands behind* GAVIN, *starts to move sensuously, slips her hands under his and starts to undo the buttons on his shirt.* GAVIN *enjoys it and starts to move with her*] Nice and slow. Play them along. Everybody? How you going?

[CRAIG *tries to perform* DAWN's *action on* BARRY, *but* BARRY *immediately throws* CRAIG's *hands away*]

BARRY: Hey! Watch it!

CRAIG: Come on, Barry!

[BARRY *grudgingly lets* CRAIG *try again.* NORMAN *is behind* RICKY, *who is anxiously looking around to see if anybody is watching*]

DAWN: Let them in. Relax and let go! Come on, fellers, think romance, think sex, think – Ladies Night!

[*Suddenly they all stop, freeze and stare, terrified, out front. The music gets louder and louder, then – blackout*]

END OF ACT ONE

ACT TWO

In the darkness we hear music: 'Macho Man'. Lights up on NORMAN *desperately rehearsing in front of full-length mirror, trying to take off shirt sexily but getting hopelessly caught up in the cuffs. He moves on and is replaced in the mirror by* RICKY *lifting weights. He drops one on his foot and hops painfully off to be replaced by* CRAIG. *He looks around, makes sure he is alone, then drops his pants. He produces a box of Man Size Tissues and starts to stuff the tissues down his underpants, realizes he has overdone it, so moves on pulling them out again.* GAVIN *comes in view with his pants round his ankles and turns round to reveal wax strips on his arse. He rips them off and lets out a silent scream. Lights up on* BARRY, *who is on his phone. We hear radio-show music. At the end of song we hear Pete Price on his Radio City late-night show.*

PETE: I've got Barry on the line now. Are you there, Barry?

BARRY: Yeah, yeah, I'm here, Pete.

PETE: Now, Barry's asking a big favour tonight. As you know I don't usually do dedications, but you've got a special request, haven't you, Barry? [BARRY *is struck dumb*] Hello, Barry, are you still there?

BARRY: Yeah, yeah, I'm still here, Pete.

PETE: So who is this special request for?

BARRY: Well, er, it's for the wife.

PETE: Does she have a name?

BARRY: Yeah, yeah, she does.

PETE: And what would her name be, Barry?

BARRY: It's Denise, Pete.

PETE: Denise. Good. See, that wasn't so difficult, was it? And how long have you and the lovely Denise been together?

BARRY: Ten years. Up until – er – last Saturday. Afternoon. About two o'clock.

PETE: Oh, there's been a lovers' tiff, has there, Barry? And you want to make it up with her on the radio? Well, why not – it's all part of the service.

BARRY: No, I mean yes – I mean, like it's a bit more serious than that. I think she's gone for good.

PETE: Oh come on, Barry, mate, don't give up so easily. That's why you've rung in, isn't it? To request a special song that means something to you both?

BARRY: Er – yeah.

PETE: So what's the message that goes to Denise with this song?

BARRY: This song's for you Denise.

PETE: Oh, you can do better than that, Barry. If you want her back, I think you'd better say those magic words – you know the three little words we can never say enough times to our loved ones.

BARRY: Oh, yeah – er – Liam misses you.

PETE: Right, well, that wasn't quite what I – let's just play your request shall we? What song do you want to dedicate to Denise, Barry?

BARRY: It's Gloria Gaynor. 'I Will Survive.'

PETE: Er – interesting choice. OK, and – er – good luck, Barry.

[*We hear 'I Will Survive' as* BARRY's *light fades to black. Lights up: we are now backstage in the show room. There is a fair-sized stage area with curtains and a "pass door" through to the auditorium. Later we will see the stage from the audience's point of view.* BARRY, GAVIN *and* NORMAN *are backstage, sorting out their costumes and props.* GAVIN *is still panicking over how he will fit into the G-string.* CRAIG *enters*]

CRAIG: Congrats, gents. Your torsos are now adorning every lamp-post and spare bit of advertising space on Merseyside.

GAVIN: Which means that, from this moment on, our arses are public property.

NORMAN: Oh, God. I'm seriously thinking about moving to Warrington.

CRAIG: Too late – I've got a mate who's been fly-posting in Warrington, Runcorn and Widnes. There's no escape from The Scouse Stallions.

BARRY: I hope Liam's mates haven't seen it anyway. Poor little bugger's got enough problems.

CRAIG: Relax, he'll think it's cool to have a famous hunky dad. Talking of hunks – where's Ricky?

NORMAN: Don't know. I haven't seen him today.

CRAIG: Shit. He knows he's supposed to be here by seven o'clock.

GAVIN: He'll be here. He's probably doing a last-minute tone-up of his muscles down the gym.

CRAIG: Or a last-minute top-up of his steroids, more like.

BARRY: How did I get myself into this?

GAVIN: [*Looking at his G-string*] And how am I going to get myself into this?

NORMAN: It's OK, Barry. It'll be a laugh.

BARRY: Yeah, you keep telling yourself that.

GAVIN: How will we know when to start?

CRAIG: Frank's going to give us the nod about ten minutes before the kick off. He's in his element. He feels he's back in show business big time. He really fancies himself as an MC.

NORMAN: MC?

CRAIG: Master of Ceremonies.

BARRY: Or in his case Miserable Cu—

CRAIG: Barry! [*Pointing to* NORMAN] Not in front of the children!

GAVIN: Is there a lighting plan?

CRAIG: Frank's sister's on the switches.

GAVIN: Oh, very high-tech!

CRAIG: Frank says she's very experienced – she works at the Echo Arena.

GAVIN: Yes, she's a bloody cleaner there.

[DAWN *enters, carrying champagne and roses*]

DAWN: Hi everybody. How are my boys feeling?

GAVIN: Much better – now our lovely boss is here.

DAWN: Ah, bless. [*Handing rose to* BARRY] Here you go, Barry.

BARRY: Ta. Nice one.

DAWN: [*Handing them round*] Norman, Gavin, Craig. I just popped in to wish you all the best. I know you'll make me proud.

CRAIG: Dawn. [*He kisses her*] What do we have here? Roses, champagne. I think we'll keep that until after the standing ovation. And then it's dinner, yeah? Tonight's the night.

DAWN: Craig —

CRAIG: No, listen. I've got so much to thank you for. You've changed my luck, turned my life around. And you look fantastic tonight, really amazing. [*He puts his arm around her, tries to embrace her, but she breaks away*]

DAWN: I'm seeing someone.

CRAIG: What?

DAWN: I'm sorry, Craig, but —

[NORMAN *comes over and puts his arm round* DAWN]

NORMAN: Thanks for the rose, doll. Nobody's ever given me flowers before.

[NORMAN *and* DAWN *kiss passionately.* CRAIG *is speechless*]

DAWN: [*To* CRAIG] We wanted to keep it quiet for professional reasons. I don't usually mix business with pleasure but, well, Norman is... very special.

CRAIG: Yes, isn't he?

DAWN: Well, I'd better go and check through the lighting with Auntie Doreen. [*Kisses* NORMAN *again*] See you later, Tiger.

[DAWN *exits and* CRAIG *stares at the jubilant* NORMAN]

NORMAN: Oh, Craig, mate, thanks for the advice. We did it. Oh, my God, it was unbelievable. You know, we did – everything. She's amazing. It was a knockout, and all thanks to you giving me that little push. I'll never forget it. You're a real mate. The best. [*He walks away*]

CRAIG: Yeah, the best. Fuck!

[FRANK *enters with a tray of drinks*]

FRANK: Here you go, lads. Compliments of the management. Just a little bit of sauce to take the edge off your nerves.

BARRY: It'd take a brewery to take the edge off mine.

[FRANK *hands out drinks, then goes into a conversation with* CRAIG. GAVIN *goes over to* BARRY, *who is sitting alone, looking at a photograph*]

GAVIN: Are you OK, Barry?

BARRY: What do you think?

GAVIN: I never thought she'd do it. Walk out on you and Liam as well. [BARRY *hands his mobile phone*] What's this?

BARRY: Denise sent me a picture message.

GAVIN: Who is it?

BARRY: A bloke from her work. She's moved in with him. Liam stayed with them last weekend.

GAVIN: She left you for this?

BARRY: Can you believe it? Must be fifty at least. Look at him – he's balding, wears glasses. For God's sake, he's fat – a real lard-arse.

GAVIN: [*Pulling his own stomach in*] Yeah, well… Have you tried to get her to come back?

BARRY: Of course I've bloody tried. Do I look like an idiot?

GAVIN: OK, OK, I only asked.

BARRY: I've tried everything. I even went on Radio City. Bared my soul to Pete Price.

GAVIN: Pete Price? I never had him down as an agony aunt.

BARRY: He played a request for me – well, I mean, for Denise, like.

GAVIN: Do you know if she heard it?

BARRY: Oh yeah, she heard it all right. She rang me up.

GAVIN: Well, that's good. [BARRY *gives him a pained look*] What did she say?

BARRY: She called me "an emotional cripple".

GAVIN: [*After a pause*] You might have done better on Jeremy Kyle.

[RICKY *bursts into the room, clutching a poster which he has ripped off a lamp post*]

RICKY: Where's that lying arsehole? Craig!

CRAIG: Oh yes, Ricky... I've been looking for you. We need to talk.

RICKY: Oh no, we don't need to talk. I'm going to sue you, you bastard. No, sorry, first I'm going to beat the shit out of you and then I'm going to sue you!

CRAIG: The poster guy screwed up. I told him not to use you – I told him. And there was no money left in the kitty to have them printed again.

RICKY: [*Tearing the poster to pieces and throwing the bits at* CRAIG] Bullshit!

CRAIG: Ricky —

RICKY: You have no idea what you've done to me, do you?

CRAIG: I really think you're over-reacting.

RICKY: Over-reacting? I haven't even started fucking reacting yet.

NORMAN: C-c-calm down, Ricky.

GAVIN: Yeah, Craig's got a point, man. I mean, it's a bit unrealistic, thinking you can become a stripper without being – well, you know – recognized.

RICKY: None of you understand. I'm a dead man. I can't ever go home again.

BARRY: Oh, come on, mate —

RICKY: I got to have street cred. I'm like Steve Gerrard round our way. Kids look up to me, you know. I'm their role model. They dress like me, they try to walk and talk like me. They think I'm a sporting hero. I'm a god in Toxteth! And then it turns out I'm just a bloody stripper.

BARRY: It's the same for all of us, Ricky. Well, apart from the role-model bit.

GAVIN: And the Toxteth god bit.

FRANK: And Steve Gerrard never pulled pints for me.

[NORMAN, BARRY, GAVIN *and* FRANK *can't suppress their laughter*]

RICKY: You're all bastards. And you – [*to* CRAIG] – you've killed me. Killed me.

CRAIG: Look, I'm sorry, man. Here, have a drink. It was an honest mistake, and I'll make it up to you somehow, I promise.

RICKY: Oh, don't worry, I'll make sure you will.

CRAIG: Now, get that down you and get yourself ready. It's gonna be a big crowd tonight, and we're depending on you.

GAVIN: A big crowd? Frank, is that true?

FRANK: We haven't sold a single ticket in the last hour.

NORMAN: Shit!

RICKY: Good.

GAVIN: [*To* FRANK] But Craig said —

FRANK: We haven't sold a ticket in the last hour because as of sixty minutes ago we had a full house – every seat is taken.

BARRY: Well, of course, we should've known. Can you imagine Frank giving us free drinks if we weren't completely sold out?

FRANK: That's right, Barry. Got it in one. [*Starts to leave but turns back*] Oh, by the way, your Denise is out there. She's brought her whole office along with her. They look a real rough bunch of slappers – but don't worry, I'll get security to keep an eye on them. [*He exits*]

BARRY: What the fuck is she playing at?

CRAIG: Take it easy. She just wants a fun night out like the rest of them.

BARRY: The bitch!

GAVIN: Maybe she's not such a bitch, Barry.

BARRY: What is she trying to do to me?

GAVIN: Calm down a minute, Barry, and think. She's going to be there, right? She's come to see you.

BARRY: Yeah, come to see me make a fool of myself!

GAVIN: No, she wants to see what she's missing.

BARRY: We've been married for ten years. She knows what she's missing!

CRAIG: OK, everybody, this is probably as good a time as any. I want to say a few words, OK? I've had a lot of ideas over the years, as you all know, and I've been here at this point before. I've seen things fall apart at the last minute too many times. But I'm determined to make this one work. That's why I'm begging you to knit together. I know, I know, we're all under pressure, we're all feeling jumpy, but please, let's make sure we don't screw this one up like everything else.

[*Before anyone can react,* GRAHAM *enters. He is exhausted, barely able to keep his eyes open and slightly drunk*]

GRAHAM: Well, here you all are. The Bootle bum boys getting ready for their debut in the wonderful world of show business.

CRAIG: What do you want, Graham? This isn't a good time —

GRAHAM: I just wanted to come and have a chat with me old mates.

CRAIG: We're in the middle of something here.

GRAHAM: Having a last-minute rehearsal?

CRAIG: A meeting actually.

GRAHAM: How about a sneak preview? Come on, you lads don't have to be shy with me. [*Wiggles his hips and starts to strip himself, he dances provocatively up to* GAVIN *and starts to undo his top button*] Nothing special about getting your kit off. I do it meself every night!

GAVIN: Get your grubby hands off me.

GRAHAM: It's not like you to complain about a little physical contact with another bloke, Gavin!

CRAIG: Graham!

GAVIN: You're a pig, Graham.

CRAIG: [*Breaking in*] How's the job in Coventry going?

GRAHAM: Great. Really great. You know, to be into some hard graft again. Honest money in your pocket, holding your head up, feeling like a real man!

GAVIN: God!

CRAIG: Long days though, with all that travelling.

GRAHAM: Don't really notice the drive – [*his eyes closing*] – get used to it, like. Oh, and they're hiring again – looking for more lads.

BARRY: Really?

GRAHAM: I'll put a word in for you, if you like.

[BARRY *and* NORMAN *look at each other, obviously interested.* CRAIG *notices*]

CRAIG: Who the hell wants to drive three hundred miles a day?

GRAHAM: Worth it – for a real job. How about it, Barry?

BARRY: I've got Liam to look after.

GRAHAM: Oh, yeah, I heard – house husband now. Poofy dancing boy by night, OXO mum by day. You're pathetic, mate. You're all pathetic.

GAVIN: Thank you for sharing your opinion with us, Graham, we're always grateful for constructive criticism. Now go fuck yourself.

GRAHAM: Don't worry, I'm off. I don't wanna hang around you pervs for too long in case it's catching.

CRAIG: Just go home, Graham.

GRAHAM: I'm going, I'm going. Don't want to be late for the show.

NORMAN: What?

GRAHAM: Yeah, I booked days ago. Brought a gang of the lads from work too. Well, we couldn't miss this one – we love a good laugh. You'll hear us.

RICKY: You're not coming, man.

GRAHAM: Oh yes, I am. So rub a bit of extra Vaseline on for me. [*He exits*]

[*They all fall silent, avoiding each other's eyes*]

CRAIG: He's bullshitting. There's no way Frank'll let him in. Forget him. Lads?

RICKY: I'm out.

BARRY: So am I.

GAVIN: Sorry, Craig —

CRAIG: Norman?

NORMAN: I can't do it on my own.

BARRY: It was a crazy idea.

CRAIG: Just like that? I don't believe you guys. Just like that? You're fucking kidding me. Two months' work and that's it? What about the money?

RICKY: Stuff the money.

BARRY: We'll have to find something else.

CRAIG: Something else? Something else? There is nothing else! That's why we were doing this in the first place. No, no, no, there is nothing else for us!!! [*Slams fist against wall*] I don't fucking believe it. Here I go again – every time, every time it goes tits up. I'm cursed. Honest to God, fucking cursed.

[*They all start to pack up.* DAWN *enters*]

DAWN: What's going on?

CRAIG: Nothing's going on. That's the point. It's all off. These no-hopers have let me down.

[CRAIG *storms out*]

DAWN: What does he mean, "it's all off"?

NORMAN: The show. We're n-n-not doing it.

DAWN: Not doing it?

NORMAN: Graham's coming along with a whole bunch of his mates.

DAWN: What of it?

NORMAN: And there are other problems – personal –

GAVIN: Barry's Denise is going to be in the audience, Ricky is pissed off because he didn't want his face on the poster and Norm – well, I'm not sure why Norm's not doing it.

NORMAN: C-c-cos nobody else is.

DAWN: I'm sorry. I'm not buying this. I thought we had a deal?

BARRY: This has nothing to do with you.

DAWN: Like hell it doesn't!

RICKY: You don't understand, OK? This is our decision. I'm sorry.

DAWN: It's not me you should be apologizing to. It's too late to cancel now. I mean, what's Frank supposed to tell that full house out there? "Sorry girls, but the lads you paid your hard-earned cash to see are having a few personal problems so it's all off." You've got to be joking!

BARRY: Look, we made a mistake, OK? Maybe we've realized too late that this isn't a job for normal men.

DAWN: And what are normal men like, Barry? Are those mates that are coming along to take the piss normal? Is that what you want to be? Like them?

Uptight women-hating slobs? God, I thought you'd
learned something here.

GAVIN: Learned how to shave our arses at least.

BARRY: The only reason people are coming is to laugh
at us.

DAWN: That's it, isn't it? I've just realized. This hasn't
got anything to do with your wife or your face
on the poster, or some mates taking the piss. No,
it's nothing to do with that. You're scared those
women aren't going to find you attractive.

RICKY: Bullshit!

DAWN: You're behaving like women yourselves. You're
scared of putting yourselves on the line in case
you're rejected.

RICKY: I'm not scared.

DAWN: Aren't you – Mr Incognito Masked Crusader?

[RICKY *backs off as* CRAIG *enters and stands quietly
at the side*]

DAWN: No, of course, you're not scared – you're terrified. All of you – terrified of opening yourselves
up. When I started this, I didn't know all the macho
rules and regulations – that it's not masculine to
pluck a single body hair, and if you stand on your
toes for more than three seconds your whole sexual

identity is in question. But – good on you, you tried. Bit by bit you really did let me drag you out of your caves and into the twenty-first century. But I was fooling myself – you're none of you man enough to risk showing your real selves to a bunch of harmless girls who just want to have a good time and celebrate their sexual freedom. Well, all I can say is – what a waste of fucking time!

[*She starts to gather her things up, collects roses and champagne, etc. and throws them all into a bin liner as she speaks*]

Barry, if you really want Denise back, you'd better start making a bit of bloody effort. And Ricky, try impressing someone over five years old. Oh, and Norman, if you can't think for yourself, don't bother to call me. And Craig, wonderboy whiz-kid Craig, call yourself a manager. You couldn't get Santa a job at Christmas!

[*She starts to leave, but turns back*]

I really thought you lot were different. Not like all the other useless men in my life. How wrong was I? Scouse Stallions? Wirral Wankers, more like! [*She exits*]

[RICKY, BARRY *and* GAVIN *resume their packing, but* NORMAN *starts towards the door after* DAWN]

CRAIG: Where are you going?

NORMAN: I'm going to tell her that I'm g-g-getting my kit off like we promised. [*He exits*]

[CRAIG *turns and looks at the others. They stop packing, look at each other*]

CRAIG: Lads?

RICKY: Oh, OK. [*Starts to undress*]

GAVIN: Can't wait. [*Gets his bag of costumes*]

CRAIG: Barry?

BARRY: Oh – why not? Fuck Denise!

CRAIG: You will, Barry. Trust me, you will!

Music: 'Crazy Horses'. Lights fade. The scene changes and we now see the stage from the audience's point of view.

AUTHORS' NOTE

At this point in the play the stage serves as the stage in a local club, and the theatre audience is assumed to be the audience at a real Ladies Night.

In some productions, Gavin is the first to appear, and does so dressed as a woman, his "drag routine" the prelude to a series of individual strip routines by each

*of the male strippers, culminating in a finale where all
the strippers and Gavin perform together.*

*What follows here, however, has Frank introducing
the strippers, delivering a comedy routine, and Gavin
is a stripper. The compère's jokes and the strip routines
change with each production to fit local tastes and
cultural references.*

* * *

[FRANK *enters, wearing a sparkling dinner jacket and
bow tie, etc. He is loving every minute of his return
to the Boards*]

FRANK: Good evening, and welcome Ladies and Gent—,
oh, sorry, hang on, Ladies and Ladies. You're all here
for an evening of culture, I can tell. I can see some of
you are our Bingo regulars – I can tell by your wings
– er, sorry, arms! Well, I think you're going to find
tonight's show a lot more stimulating than playing
numbers with a table full of pensioners. And, who
knows, if you hang around afterwards, you might
just hit the jackpot! So this is it, girls. You're going
to see the real thing tonight. Forget about those
pumped up, silicone-enhanced foreigners with their
fake tans. Tonight you're going to see genuine raw
Merseyside meat. The boys next door, getting their

kit off just for you – the girls next door. Unless you live next to a convent, of course. First up we have Barry. Some of you may have known him when he was winding back the mileage clock on Japanese imports, but he's not doing that any more. Tonight he's here to get your engines revving. So a big welcome, please, for Barry the ballsy biker!

[BARRY's *routine. Music: 'Sex Bomb'.* BARRY *rides in on his motorcycle, beaming his headlight around the audience. He gets off the bike and starts to strip. When he gets his leather jacket off, he turns and reveals the back of his T-shirt, which reads: "I love you, Denise". Once he is down to a jockstrap, a bubble bath appears. He gets in, takes off his jockstrap, wrings it out, then throws it to the floor as the bath is drawn offstage*]

[FRANK *returns, picking up the jockstrap as he enters*]

FRANK: [*Throwing it out front*] There you go, love. See if you can get that filled by next Friday! Actually, I recognize you, don't I? We had sex last week round the back of the chippie. We did. I told her I love it when women talk dirty to me. She said, "OK, in that case, get off me you fat bastard!" Oh yes, she's a real lady. Now, you'll like this next one, girls. But you've got to be gentle with him. He's a bit shy, so

you'll have to give him a hand. Get back, woman!
You'll scare the poor fuc— feller. Let's hear it for
Norman the Fireman!

[NORMAN's *routine. Music: 'Sex on Fire' (Kings of Leon). Smoke, flashing lights, flames and alarms are followed by* NORMAN, *dressed as a fireman, sliding down a pole. He strips, does some pole-dancing, then strips some more and picks up a large fire hose, with which he mimes putting out the flames and soaking the audience. As he takes off his G-string, he disappears into the onstage flames*]

[FRANK *comes back*]

FRANK: Well, I can see Norman lit a few fires out
there. Get some more liquor down you, girls, try
to cool down. And talking of cool, next up we have
Mr Cool himself. He's going to take you right up in
the sky – sorry, I mean take you right up to the sky.
Come and fly with him – or vice versa. Here's your
cabin crew for the night – it's Gavin the Frequent
F-Flyer!

[GAVIN's *routine. Music: 'The Stripper'.* GAVIN *enters, dressed as an airline steward and pushing a trolley. He mimes safety instructions while removing his clothing. He then demonstrates the life vest, provocatively inflating it, etc. with his mouth. He distributes "duty free" goods, taking cash and cards in return for the rest of his own clothing. He ends up wearing only the safety vest with his crotch concealed by a sick bag]*

[FRANK *re-enters*]

FRANK: And he gives Air Miles as well, so you'll collect some points from him, I'll bet. OK, next up is the guy whose idea this whole thing was, so if you're not enjoying yourselves he's the one to have it out with. And, believe me, he has no problems getting it out. Tonight he's bringing you a taste of the Wild West. No, love, not West Derby! It's the land of the ambushes, the saloon-bar brawls, the wild vigilantes – on second thoughts, maybe it is West Derby. He's riding in across the Prairie now, just for you. And yes, that is a gun in his pocket and, yes, he is also pleased to see you. It's Cowboy Craig.

[CRAIG's *routine. Music: 'Here You Come Again'.* CRAIG, *dressed as a cowboy, enters through swinging saloon-bar doors. After a few passes with his lasso, he twirls his guns and then starts to strip. Under his shirt he has two sheriff's badges covering his nipples. He is wearing chaps over his jeans, and when he rips his jeans off his chaps remain and we see he has another sheriff's star covering his crotch. He turns, exposes his bare bum and walks slowly out of the saloon door*]

[FRANK *re-enters*]

FRANK: Is everybody still breathing? Any casualties? Well, hold tight girls, this could be the one to finish you off – if you know what I mean. He's a man of mystery – nobody knows who he is or where he's come from. But I know where you'd like him to go. Hang on to your hats, girls – it's El Zorro!

[RICKY's *routine. Music: 'Smooth' (Santana). Sound effect of swishing sword is followed by* RICKY *swinging onto the stage at the end of a rope, wearing a mask and dressed as Zorro. He leaps from the rope and mimes sword-fighting. Around his waist he has a length of red silk which he throws to a woman in the audience* (PLANT) *Still attached to the silk he spins away from her and then pulls himself back towards her, eventually drawing her up onto the stage. He then strips for her alone. He is eventually wearing only his cloak and G-string. He covers her with his cloak and she emerges clutching her trophy – his G-string. She staggers back to her seat*]

[FRANK *returns*]

FRANK: Well, that's the last we'll see of her for a bit. She'll be polishing Zorro's sword for weeks. Now, I'm happy to announce that, as tonight's been a sellout and we've had to turn a lot of disappointed customers away, The Scouse Stallions will be appearing here every month from now on. And don't forget that the end of the show is not the end of the fun. The bar will be open for more liquid refreshments and a large selection of gourmet snacks, including pies, pasties and sausage rolls. Right, well that's nearly it. You've seen what you came for. What? You haven't? OK, if you insist. Here comes the Big One. Not one, not two, three or four, but five strapping lads – the pick of Mersey Manhood. I give you... our grand finale with the five and only Scouse Stallions!

[*The final strip. Music: 'Simply Irresistible' (Robert Palmer).* CRAIG, BARRY, NORMAN, RICKY *and* GAVIN *enter dressed as construction workers with tools, hard hats, etc. They have obviously been working hard. Their act is polished and precise and beautifully choreographed. They slowly strip down to their famous jewelled G-strings. They turn their backs on the audience, rip their G-strings off and walk in a straight line upstage. When they reach the back wall, they pick up their hats and cover themselves before they turn, look at the audience, then look at each other.* CRAIG *gives them the nod, and with perfect timing they throw their arms and their hats in the air*]

[*Blackout. The walkdown. Music: 'It's Raining Men'.* DAWN *dances. She is joined by* FRANK *and then by all the guys* [*including* GRAHAM], *who are now wearing transparent raincoats. Bows.*]

THE END